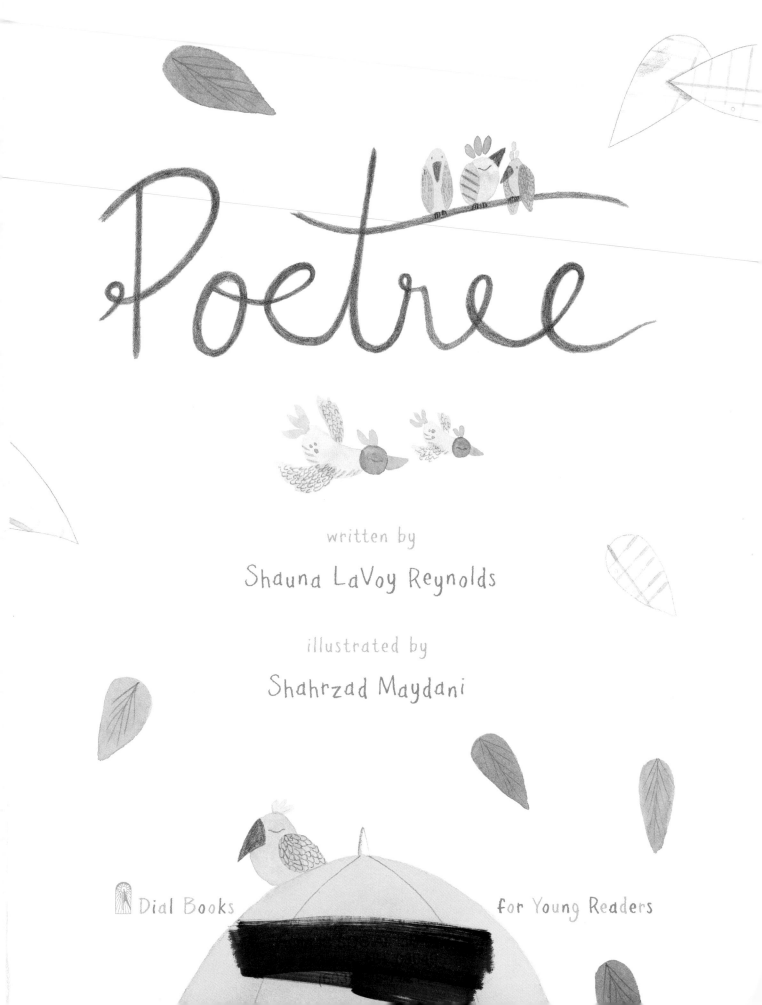

Poetree

written by

Shauna LaVoy Reynolds

illustrated by

Shahrzad Maydani

Dial Books   for Young Readers

The snow had melted, the buttercups were blooming, and Sylvia celebrated winter's end by writing a poem about spring.

She walked with Shel to the park at the
top of the hill and read it to a squirrel:

Spring is here at last.

I hope it doesn't end too fast.

Like a bee I'll sniff each flower,

And I'll enjoy each springy hour

(So much).

The squirrel seemed grateful. Sylvia tied her poem to a birch tree and headed home, hoping that it didn't count as littering if it made the world more splendid.

The next morning Sylvia passed the birch on her way to school. From a distance she saw her poem fluttering in the breeze.

But when she got closer she realized that it wasn't her poem at all:

I think spring is the best of the seasons
For plenty of excellent reasons—
Like birdy parents building nests
Where all the baby birds can rest
(And play).

Sylvia's heart did a somersault.
She never imagined the tree
might write back.

In class, Sylvia daydreamed
about her new leafy friend.

"SYLVIA, please pay attention," said Ms. Oliver.

"Yeah, Sylvia," whispered Walt, the boy sitting behind
her. Their classmates giggled, and Sylvia sank in her seat.

After lunch, Ms. Oliver taught the class about haiku.

Sylvia struggled to contain her excitement in seventeen syllables.

White birch on the hill

Speaks out loud through rustling leaves

Great green Poetree

Ms. Oliver gave Sylvia a gold star.

When the bell rang, Sylvia ran straight to the Poetree.
She folded her haiku into a paper boat and pushed it
halfway into a knothole.

"So, what's your name?"
   Sylvia asked the tree.
   But the tree stood in silence.

"Are you shy like me?"
   The tree nodded in the breeze.
   Sylvia understood.

That night Sylvia dreamed of rhymes
falling like autumn leaves.

She dreamed of cheerful songbirds
greeting her in perfect rhythm.

On Saturday morning Sylvia rushed to the park with a heart full of hope. The knothole was empty, and she saw no notes on the branches. But the whisper of the wind in the leaves above her was like a poem.

Sylvia looked up and saw fragments of sky peeking through the treetop. She spoke the words as they blossomed into her mind:

Sky so blue, grass so green,
Tree so tall in between.
Favorite friend in morning light
And under moon glow late at night.

Sylvia selected a twig from the ground and gripped it like a pencil. "By Sylvia" she wrote in the air, but that didn't seem right.

"LOVE, Sylvia." She waved her stick with a flourish, accidentally hitting a branch.

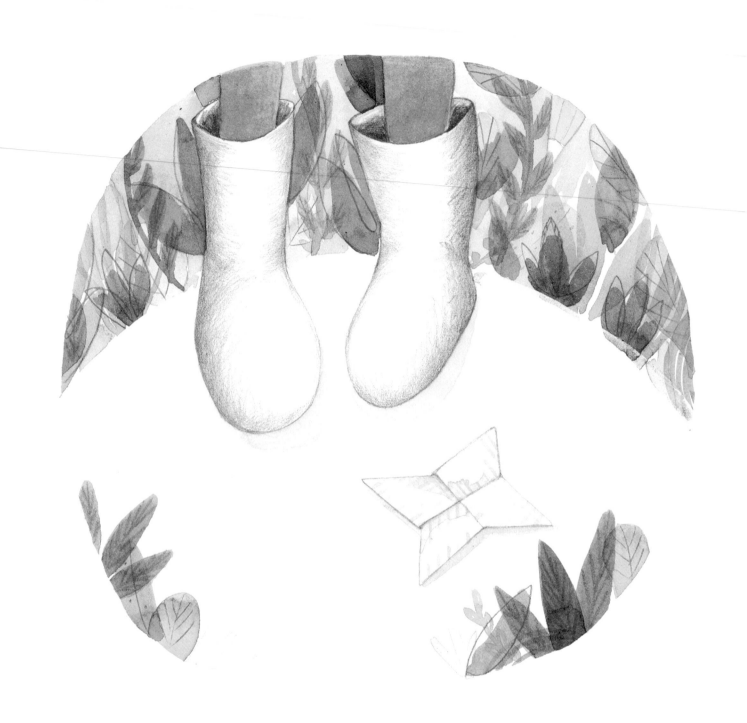

A tightly folded ninja star fell to her feet.
Sylvia couldn't unfold it fast enough:

I've wondered a while
Can a tree and child be friends?
Your words give me hope.

Sylvia felt a spark in her heart. Good thing she
brought sidewalk chalk. She scrawled in big
blocky letters so the birch could see:

I never thought that I would see
Such lovely poems from a tree.
I wish that I could climb and live
Among the words you love to give.
But if I lived up in a tree
I sure would miss my family
(Especially Shel).

Sylvia thought it was the greatest thing she had
written in all her years. She wrapped her arms
around the Poetree.

It was stronger, wiser, and kinder than the children at school.
She knew she would always have a friend at the park.

She didn't open her eyes until Shel barked.

Walt was there, staring at the ninja star haiku sticking
out of Sylvia's pocket.

"That's not for you. That's for my tree."

Sylvia blinked. "It was from the tree. Just for me."

Walt shook his head.

Sylvia didn't understand. Had the tree she loved so much
not given her a thing?

Sylvia didn't want to cry.

Not at the park.

Walt didn't want her to cry, either.

"I'm sorry I was mean at school," he said.

Sylvia smiled.

"A friend of the tree is okay with me."
She could never resist a good rhyme.

Walt read Sylvia's chalk poem out loud.

"You're a wonderful poet," he said.
"You deserved that gold star. But who is Shel?"

Sylvia pointed.
"My best friend's name is Shel. I think he likes
the way you smell."

"I can tell!" added Walt.

The two poets giggled.

"Can I borrow your chalk?"

Walt composed a new poem next to Sylvia's:

If you want to share a poem with me,
Give it to the tall birch tree.
Or if you need a friend for writing,
Playing with, or sit beside-ing,
I'll be here for you joyfully,
Right beneath the Poetree.

The new friends sat a while, side by side, backs against the birch. Sunlight and shadows danced through the leaves above them as they silently searched for the most marvelous words to describe it all.

For David, Siri, and Judah—
three bright sparks in my heart
—S.L.R.

For my two little birds
—S.M.

Dial Books for Young Readers
An imprint of Penguin Random House LLC, New York

Text copyright © 2019 by Shauna LaVoy Reynolds
Illustrations copyright © 2019 by Shahrzad Maydani

Visit us online at Penguinrandomhouse.com

ISBN 9780399539121

Printed in China

1 3 5 7 9 10 8 6 4 2

Design by Mina Chung • Text set in Stempel Garamond and Pencil Pete
This art was created by using graphite pencil and watercolors.